Puppy Mudge Takes a Bath

By Cynthia Rylant

Illustrated by Isidre Moñes

in the style of Suçie Stevenson

Ready-to-Read

Simon Spotlight
New York   London   Toronto   Sydney   New Delhi

This is Henry.

This is Henry's puppy Mudge.
Mudge loves mud.

Mud makes Mudge roll.

And roll.
And roll.

Mudge is muddy.
Mudge needs a bath.

There is the tub.

Where is Mudge?

Mudge is hiding.
Mudge does not love tubs.

Henry finds Mudge.

Mudge is in the tub.

Now Henry is in the tub!
Mudge is happy.

Mudge is very clean.
Henry is very clean.

The tub is very muddy!

Henry and Mudge dry off.
They go back outside.

Look what Mudge found.

Mudge is smelly.

Mudge needs a bath.

There is the tub.

Where is Mudge?

Here we go again.

Puppy Mudge Wants to Play

By Cynthia Rylant

Illustrated by Suçie Stevenson

Ready-to-Read

Simon Spotlight
New York   London   Toronto   Sydney   New Delhi

This is Henry's puppy, Mudge.
Mudge wants to play.

Henry is reading.
Henry does not want to play.

Mudge cannot read.

Mudge wants to play.

Mudge pulls off Henry's sock.

"Aw, Mudge," says Henry.

Henry reads.

Mudge chews up Henry's laces.

"Aw, Mudge," says Henry.

Henry reads.
Mudge sits on Henry's foot.

Mudge sits on Henry's lap.

Mudge sits on Henry's book.
Mudge looks at Henry.

Mudge looks and looks and looks at Henry.
"Mudge," asks Henry, "do you want to play?"

Mudge jumps.
Mudge dances.

Mudge goes round and round.

Mudge WANTS TO PLAY.

So they do!

Puppy Mudge Has a Snack

By Cynthia Rylant

Illustrated by Isidre Mones

in the style of Suçie Stevenson

Ready-to-Read

Simon Spotlight
New York   London   Toronto   Sydney   New Delhi

This is Mudge.

He is Henry's puppy.

Mudge wants Henry's snack.

Mudge gets on Henry's lap.

"No, Mudge," says Henry.

Mudge wants Henry's snack.

Mudge gets on Henry's head.

Mudge wants Henry's snack.

Mudge drools.

"Aw, Mudge," says Henry.

Mudge looks cute.

Mudge looks very, very cute.

Mudge looks too cute.

"Mudge, you are TOO cute," says Henry.

Henry gets a snack for Mudge.
It is a CRACKER.

Mudge LOVES crackers.

Now Henry has a snack.
And Mudge has a snack.

And all Mudge had to be was
CUTE!

Puppy Mudge Loves His Blanket

By Cynthia Rylant

Illustrated by Isidre Mones

in the style of Suçie Stevenson

Ready-to-Read

Simon Spotlight
New York   London   Toronto   Sydney   New Delhi

This is Mudge.
He is Henry's puppy.

Mudge has a blanket.

Mudge LOVES his blanket.

He sleeps on it.

He hides under it.

He takes it places.

Sometimes he loses it.

Where is Mudge's blanket now?

Henry looks on the chair.

Mudge looks on the chair.
No blanket.

Henry looks under the bed.
Mudge looks under the bed.

No blanket.

Mudge sniffs.

He sniffs and sniffs and sniffs.

Good Mudge!
He sniffed all the way . . .

to his blanket!

Now he can rest.

Puppy Mudge Finds a Friend

By Cynthia Rylant

Illustrated by Suçie Stevenson

Ready-to-Read

Simon Spotlight
New York   London   Toronto   Sydney   New Delhi

This is Puppy Mudge.
He lives with Henry.

Mudge likes it.

He likes a lot of things.

He likes chew toys.

He likes crackers.

He likes to drool.

(Mudge drools a lot.)

Mudge also likes cats.

Mudge found a cat friend.

Mudge and Fluffy play.

Fluffy hides.

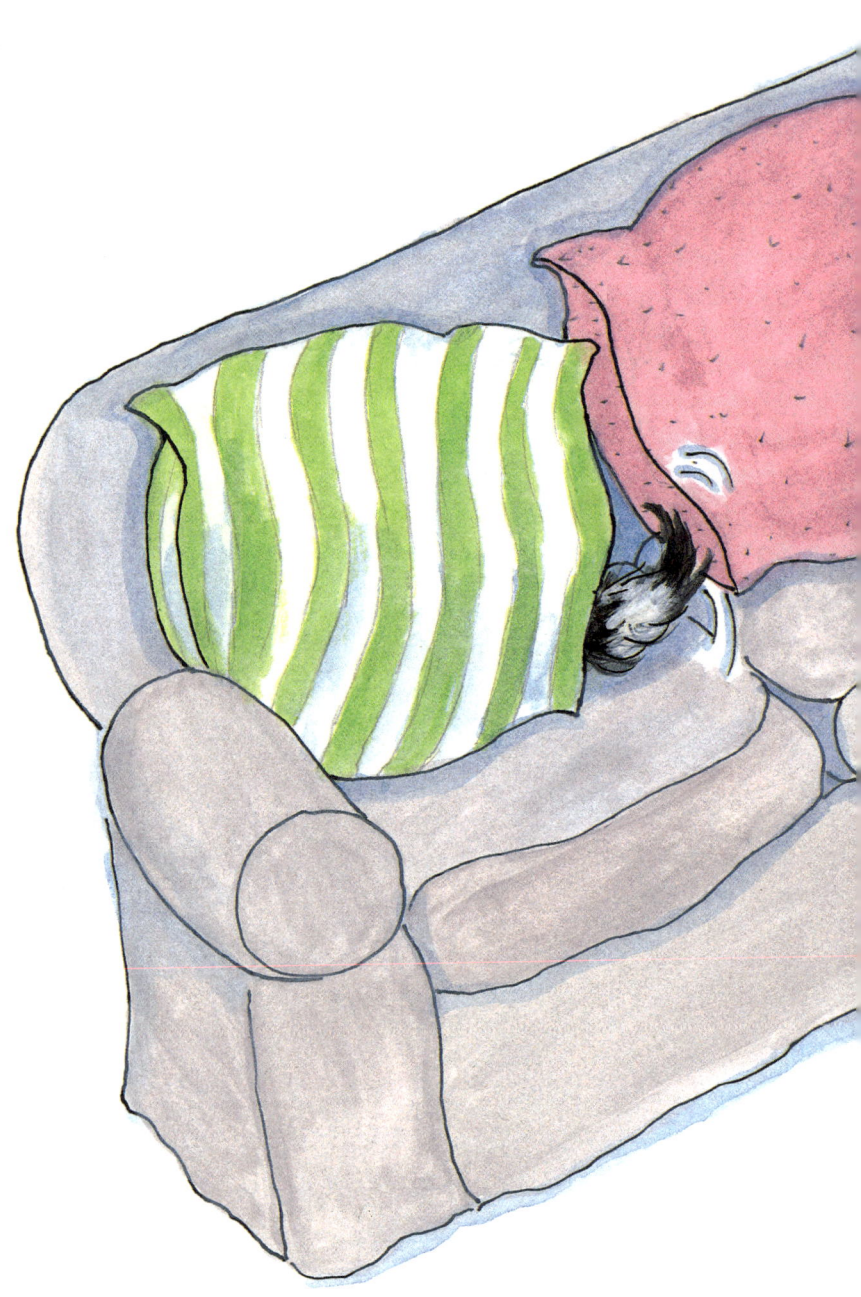

Mudge hides.

Mudge does not.

Fluffy and Mudge play and play.

Then they rest.

Fluffy purrs.
Mudge snores.

Friends.

Henry and Mudge

The First Book of Their Adventures

Story by Cynthia Rylant
Pictures by Suçie Stevenson

Ready-to-Read

Simon Spotlight
New York   London   Toronto   Sydney

Contents

Henry	5
Mudge	9
Henry	14
Mudge	18
Mudge	23
Henry	28
Henry and Mudge	35

Henry

Henry had no brothers
and no sisters.
"I want a brother,"
he told his parents.
"Sorry," they said.
Henry had no friends
on his street.

"I want to live
on a different street,"
he told his parents.
"Sorry," they said.
Henry had no pets
at home.
"I want to have a dog,"
he told his parents.
"Sorry," they *almost* said.

But first they looked
at their house
with no brothers and sisters.
Then they looked
at their street
with no children.
Then they looked
at Henry's face.

Then they looked at each other.

"Okay," they said.

"I want to hug you!"

Henry told his parents.

And he did.

Mudge

Henry searched for a dog.

"Not just any dog," said Henry.

"Not a short one," he said.

"Not a curly one," he said.

"And no pointed ears."

Then he found Mudge.
Mudge had floppy ears,
not pointed.
And Mudge had straight fur,
not curly.
But Mudge was short.
"Because he's a puppy,"
Henry said.
"He'll grow."

And did he ever!

He grew out of his puppy cage.

He grew out of his dog cage.

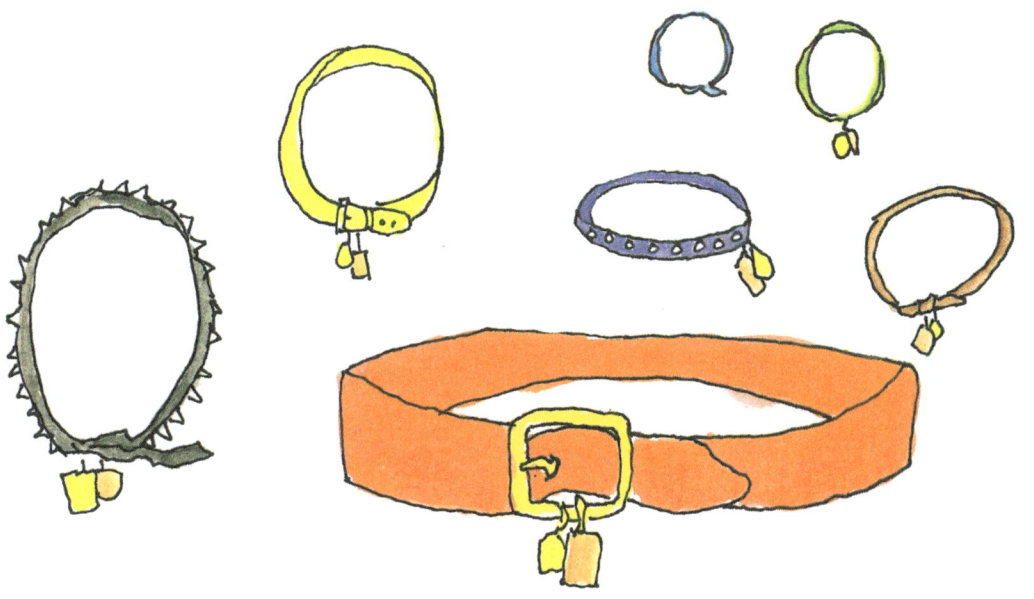

He grew out of seven collars
in a row.
And when he finally
stopped growing . . .

he weighed one hundred eighty pounds,
he stood three feet tall,
and he drooled.
"I'm glad you're not short,"
Henry said.

And Mudge licked him,
then sat on him.

Henry

Henry used to walk
to school alone.
When he walked
he used to worry about
tornadoes,
ghosts,
biting dogs,
and bullies.

He walked as fast
as he could.
He looked straight ahead.
He never looked back.
But now he walked to school
with Mudge.

And now when he walked,
he thought about
vanilla ice cream,
rain,
rocks,
and good dreams.
He walked to school
but not too fast.
He walked to school
and sometimes backward.

He walked to school
and patted Mudge's big head,
happy.

Mudge

Mudge loved Henry's room.

He loved the dirty socks.

He loved the stuffed bear.

He loved the fish tank.

But mostly he loved

Henry's bed.

Because in Henry's bed
was Henry.
Mudge loved to climb in
with Henry.
Then he loved
to smell him.

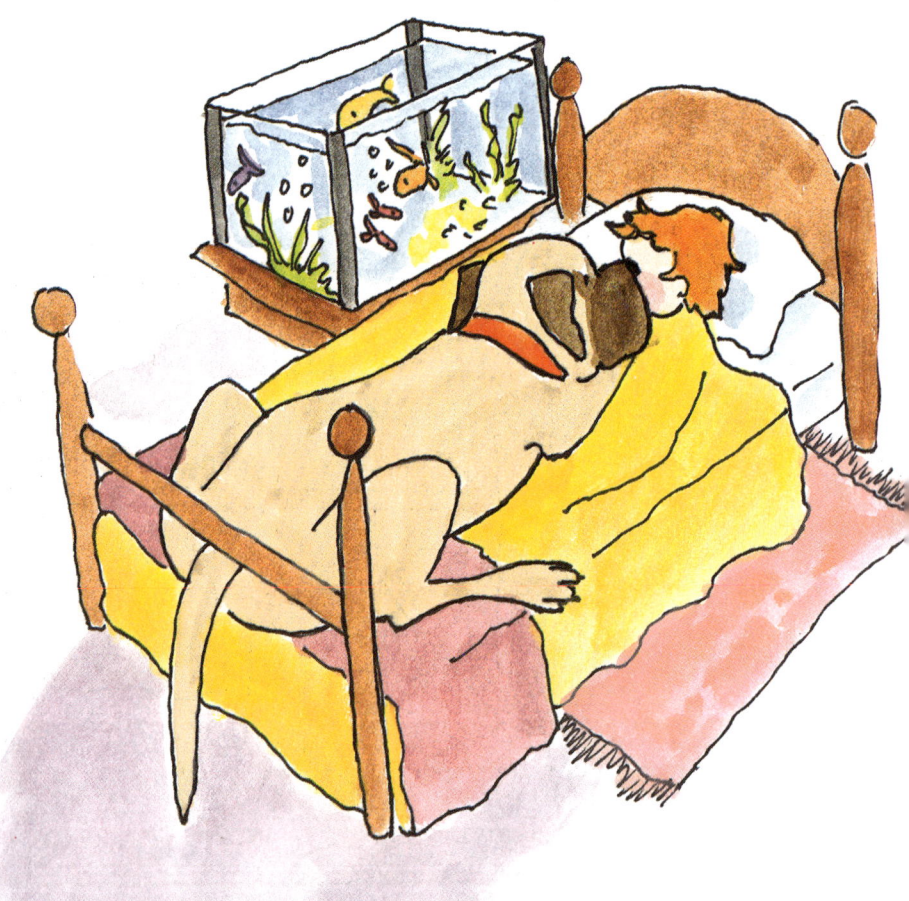

He smelled his lemon hair.

He smelled his milky mouth.

He smelled his soapy ears.

He smelled his chocolate fingers.

Then he put his head
by Henry's head.
He looked at the fish tank.
He looked at the bear.
He looked at Henry.
He licked him.
And he fell asleep.

Mudge

One day Mudge took a walk

without Henry.

The sun was shining,

the birds were flying,

the grass smelled sweet.

Mudge couldn't wait for Henry.

So he left.

He went down one road,

sniffing the bushes,

then down another road,

kicking up dust.

He went through a field,

across a stream,

into some pine trees.

And when he came out
on the other side,
he was lost.

He couldn't smell Henry.
He couldn't smell
his front porch.
He couldn't smell
the street he lived on.
Mudge looked all around
and didn't see anything
or anyone
he knew.

He whined a little,
alone without Henry.
Then he lay down,
alone without Henry.
He missed Henry's bed.

Henry

Henry thought Mudge
would be with him always.
He thought Mudge
made everything safe.
He thought Mudge
would never go away.

And when Mudge did go away,
when Henry called and called
but Mudge didn't come,
Henry's heart hurt
and he cried for an hour.
But when he finished crying,
Henry said, "Mudge loves me.
He wouldn't leave.
He must be lost."

So Henry walked and walked,
and he called and called,
and he looked and looked
for his dog Mudge.
He walked down one road,
then down another road.
The sun shone as Henry ran
through a field,
calling and calling.

The birds flew past
as he stood beside a stream,
calling and calling.

And the tears fell again
as he looked at the
empty pine trees
for his lost dog.
"*Mudge!*" he called, one last time.

And Mudge woke up
from his lonely sleep,
then
came
running.

Henry and Mudge

Every day when Henry woke up,

he saw Mudge's big head.

And every day

when Mudge woke up,

he saw Henry's small face.

They ate breakfast
at the same time;

they ate supper
at the same time.

And when Henry was at school,
Mudge just lay around
and waited.
Mudge never went for a walk
without Henry again.
And Henry never worried
that Mudge would leave.

Because sometimes, in their dreams,
they saw long silent roads,
big wide fields,
deep streams,
and pine trees.

In those dreams,
Mudge was alone
and Henry was alone.
So when Mudge woke up
and knew Henry was with him,
he remembered the dream
and stayed closer.

And when Henry woke up
and knew Mudge was with him,
he remembered the dream
and the looking
and the calling
and the fear
and he knew
he would never lose Mudge
again.